PUFFIN BOO

Not Quite a Mermaid
MERMAID FIRE

Linda Chapman lives in Leicestershire with her
family and two Bernese mountain dogs. When
she is not writing she spends her time looking after
her two young daughters, horse riding and
teaching drama.

Books by Linda Chapman

MY SECRET UNICORN series
NOT QUITE A MERMAID series
STARDUST series

BRIGHT LIGHTS
CENTRE STAGE

Not Quite a Mermaid
MERMAID FIRE

LINDA CHAPMAN

Illustrated by Dawn Apperley

PUFFIN

To Charlotte and Beatrix Ambery and Lucy Proudman
for playing mermaids one Easter holiday and giving me
the idea about Electra in the first place

PUFFIN BOOKS

Published by the Penguin Group
Penguin Books Ltd, 80 Strand, London WC2R 0RL, England
Penguin Group (USA) Inc., 375 Hudson Street, New York, New York 10014, USA
Penguin Group (Canada), 10 Alcorn Avenue, Toronto, Ontario, Canada M4V 3B2 (a division of
Pearson Penguin Canada Inc.)
Penguin Ireland, 25 St Stephen's Green, Dublin 2, Ireland
(a division of Penguin Books Ltd)
Penguin Group (Australia), 250 Camberwell Road, Camberwell, Victoria 3124, Australia (a
division of Pearson Australia Group Pty Ltd)
Penguin Books India Pvt Ltd, 11 Community Centre, Panchsheel Park,
New Delhi – 110 017, India
Penguin Group (NZ), cnr Airborne and Rosedale Roads, Albany, Auckland 1310, New
Zealand (a division of Pearson New Zealand Ltd)
Penguin Books (South Africa) (Pty) Ltd, 24 Sturdee Avenue, Rosebank, Johannesburg 2196,
South Africa

Penguin Books Ltd, Registered Offices: 80 Strand, London WC2R 0RL, England

www.penguin.com

First published 2005
5

Text copyright © Linda Chapman, 2005
Illustrations copyright © Dawn Apperley, 2005
All rights reserved

The moral right of the author and illustrator has been asserted

Set in Palatino
Made and printed in England by Clays Ltd, St Ives plc

British Library Cataloguing in Publication Data
A CIP catalogue record for this book is available from the British Library

Contents

Chapter One

'I want to do something exciting,' Electra the mermaid declared. She looked at the nearby rock that jutted out of the bright blue sea. 'I know! I'm going to dive off Turtle Rock and see if I can swim all the way down to the seabed.'

Sam and Sasha, the mer-twins, stared at her. They lived in the next-door cave to Electra and the three of them often played together.

'You mustn't!' Sasha exclaimed, swishing her long silver tail. 'The sea's really deep round Turtle Rock.'

'I'll be OK,' Electra replied.

'But you don't know what will be

down there,' Sam protested. 'There might be all sorts of dangerous sea creatures. No one ever dives down that far, Electra.'

'That's why it will be exciting.' Electra grinned.

She saw the confusion on the twins' faces and sighed. Sam and Sasha just didn't understand. Like all the other merchildren who lived in the sea round Mermaid Island, the twins never wanted to do anything daring. They were quite happy just swimming in the shallows and playing on the coral reef that encircled the island. Even the adult merpeople liked staying safe and keeping out of trouble. But Electra was different. She longed for adventure.

She looked over to where a young dolphin was bobbing up and down in the sea. 'Are you coming with me, Splash?' she called.

Splash dived under the water and surfaced beside her. 'Of course I am!'

Splash's parents had died and now he lived with Electra and her mum, Maris. He was Electra's best friend and he loved having adventures just as much as she did.

'Come on then,' she said to him. And ignoring the twins' worried faces, she swam over to Turtle Rock. As she pulled herself out of the water, her feet slipped slightly on the damp stone. While all the other merpeople who lived on the coral reef had long silvery tails, Electra had two legs. It was because she hadn't been born a mermaid; she had been born a human.

One night, eight years ago, there

had been a terrible storm. After it had finally passed, the merpeople saw a battered boat floating out in the deep sea. Everyone thought that the boat was empty, but then Maris heard a strange noise and swam over to investigate. She found Electra inside the boat. At the time, Electra had been just a tiny baby. The merpeople had rescued her and brought her up as a mermaid, giving her magic sea powder so she could breathe underwater. Maris had adopted her and become her mum. Now, Electra couldn't imagine being anything but a mermaid. She couldn't swim as fast as the other mermaids, but otherwise she did everything they did. Well, apart from being good and doing as she was told, of course. But then, being sensible was just so boring!

Taking a deep breath, Electra dived into the turquoise water.

Down she went, the water blurring around her in a stream of green and blue. Feeling herself slow down, she kicked with her feet. She wasn't going to stop until she reached the very bottom. Glancing to one side, she saw Splash beside her.

They reached the seabed. Shoals of orange and blue fish swam past them. Brightly coloured sea cucumbers clung to rocks and clusters of rose coral grew in the sand. Even though this was one of the deepest points in the sea round Mermaid Island, the water was still shallow enough for sunlight to filter through. Swimming in the warm water, Electra felt disappointed. Everything looked

pretty much the same as it did on the coral reef. The most exciting thing was a giant clam wedged between two rocks, its blue mouth snapping shut as they swam past.

She turned to Splash. 'There's nothing very scary down here.'

'I guess it's just not deep enough,' Splash replied. 'It would be different if we were swimming outside the reef.'

'Maybe tomorrow we'll get a chance to dive really deep,' Electra said hopefully. A shiver of excitement ran through her. The very next day at school, her class was going to have their first lesson in collecting mermaid fire – a magic underwater fire that came from the coral reef and the seabed. The merpeople used it for cooking and heating things up. Electra couldn't wait to learn how to

collect it, particularly because this meant going out into the deep sea beyond the safety of the coral reef.

'Yes, tomorrow we'll be able to swim out and dive really far down,' Splash said eagerly.

Electra nodded, her eyes shining at the thought. 'Come on,' she said. 'There's nothing to see here. Let's go back to the others.'

'Electra! Splash!' Sam exclaimed anxiously as they swam up to the surface. 'Are you OK?'

'Of course,' Electra replied, pushing her long red hair back from her face.

'Did you see anything exciting down there?' Sasha asked, her eyes wide.

Electra sighed. 'No. There was just the usual sort of thing: fish, seaweed and coral. But tomorrow's going to be different. I'm going to dive really deep then.'

Sasha shivered. 'You're mad. I'm

going to stay as close to the reef as possible. What if some sharks come again?'

The last time Electra had been out into the deep sea, Sam and Sasha had gone too, and sharks had almost eaten all of them.

'The teachers are going to watch out for any sharks,' Electra said. 'We'll be fine. Collecting mermaid fire is going to be so exciting.'

'I bet you'll be really good at it, Electra,' Sam said. 'Mum told me that the deeper you dive, the more you get.'

Electra nodded excitedly. She had heard that too and she was already determined that she was going to be the one to collect the most fire the next day.

Just then, there was a shout. 'Sam! Sasha!' It was the twins' dad, Ronan, calling to them from near the coral reef. 'Supper time!'

'Coming, Dad!' the twins called back.

Electra glanced at the sun. It was starting to sink towards the sea, turning the sky purple and pink. 'We'd better get going too,' she said to

Splash. 'Mum will be cross if we're late.' She turned to the others. 'See you tomorrow at school.'

'Yeah, see you,' they called.

Electra and Splash set off through the water. 'I think tomorrow's going to be fun,' Splash said to Electra.

She grinned at him. 'I bet it is!' she replied.

Chapter Two

'Now, promise me you'll be good,' Maris said the following morning as Electra picked up her school bag and swam to the cave entrance with Splash.

Electra grinned. 'I'm always good!'

Maris raised her eyebrows. 'Hmmm.'

'I'll be careful, Mum,' Electra said. 'Don't worry!' She and Splash swam out of the cave.

Electra's school was halfway up the reef. Stony coral formed benches and tables where the mergirls and merboys sat for their lessons.

'I'll stay over here till you go out to find some mermaid fire,' Splash said to Electra as they neared the school. Solon, Electra's teacher, didn't like pets coming to school. None of Electra's friends had a dolphin as a pet but plenty had sea horses and sea slugs, and Solon got very cross when they brought them to class. 'I'll jump out over the coral reef to join you when you swim into the deep sea,' Splash said.

Electra nodded. 'OK. I'll see you later.' She gave him a hug and then swam over to join her friends.

The morning seemed to drag by. Electra just couldn't concentrate on adding up cowrie shells and braiding seaweed into necklaces. All she could think about was getting out into the deep sea and learning how to collect

mermaid fire.

When Solon eventually led them out through the white gate in the coral reef, Electra couldn't wait to get started. She plunged eagerly through the gate and out into the deep sea.

'It feels really weird to be out here,' Sam said, looking around.

Sasha shivered. 'I don't like it. It's too big.'

'How can you not like it?' Electra exclaimed. 'It's amazing!' Excitement raced through her. Everything seemed so vast and huge outside the reef.

Just then, a grey shape came leaping over the reef.

'Splash!' Electra said in delight. She swam over to where Splash had dived into the water.

'Hi,' he said, bobbing up beside her.

Nearby, four older mermaids were

conducting a survey on jellyfish. They looked about ten years old. They glanced at Electra and her friends.

'Ah, look, it's the Year Fours,' one of the mermaids said. She had long blonde hair tied back in a thick plait. 'I bet it's their first time out in the deep sea.' She grinned at her friends. 'They're so little. Don't they look sweet?'

One of the other mermaids laughed. She had long brown hair tied back in an almost identical plait. 'And scared. I bet they're dreading diving into the sea.'

21

Electra frowned. She didn't like being called little and sweet and she certainly wasn't scared.

Sam swam over and pulled her arm. 'Come on, Electra,' he said, looking around. 'Solon's calling everyone together.'

He and Sasha started to swim over to where the class was gathering. But Electra stayed where she was. She glared at the older mermaids. 'I'm not scared!'

'Yeah, right.' The first mermaid laughed.

'I'm not!' Electra said hotly. 'I like diving. In fact, I bet I can dive as deep as any of you!'

'As if,' said the mermaid with brown hair. 'We're the best divers in our year. We've dived almost all the way to the seabed. And it's really scary down there.'

'Well, I could dive that far too!' Electra said indignantly.

'Electra!'

Hearing her teacher's sharp voice, Electra swung round.

Solon was swimming towards her, his face angry. 'I've called you three times. Now, will you please come over and join the others!'

Electra glanced towards where the rest of her class were gathered in obedient rows and felt her face going pink. She'd been so busy arguing with the older mermaids that she hadn't even heard Solon calling her.

'Honestly, Electra!' Solon said crossly as they swam to join the others. 'We haven't even started collecting fire and already you're not paying attention. I've a good mind to send you back to the reef.'

Electra looked at him in alarm. 'I'll be good. I promise!' She couldn't bear the thought of being sent back.

'All right,' Solon said. 'But you must concentrate.'

Electra quickly swam over to join Sam and Sasha.

'Where's Splash?' Sam whispered.

Electra looked around. 'I don't know,' she replied in a low voice. 'Keeping out of Solon's way, I hope.'

'OK, Class Four, listen carefully,' Solon began. 'As you know, today you're going to learn how to collect mermaid fire. It can only be collected by touching your hands to either coral or rocks on the seabed, and saying these magic words.' He held out his hands. 'From the deep of the sea,' he said, his voice rising commandingly, 'mermaid fire come to me!'

Just then, a grey head popped out

of the water beside him. Solon spluttered in surprise. The class giggled.

'Splash!' Electra exclaimed.

Splash clicked his tongue and looked at her happily.

Solon looked furious. 'Electra!' he bellowed. 'Get that dolphin out of here!'

Electra called Splash over. Realizing he had got her into trouble, Splash looked upset. 'I'm sorry, Electra,' he said as they swam over to the gate. 'I didn't realize I was going to come up right beside Solon.'

'It's OK.' Electra sighed. 'But you'd better go home. Solon's really mad.'

'I don't want to go home,' Splash protested.

'I know,' Electra said, feeling mean. 'But you can't stay around here. Solon will send me home if he sees you again.'

'OK,' Splash agreed. 'I'll see you later then.' Electra nodded and swam back to the others. They had all started to practise the magic spell. She quickly joined in. The words were very easy to remember.

'Very good, everyone,' Solon said,

after they had been practising for a while. 'I think you're ready to have a go at collecting fire. Just dive down, put your hands on the reef and say the magic words.'

Electra dived eagerly into the sea and swam to a piece of the reef. She put her hand on the hard stony coral. This was it. Her first chance to collect mermaid fire! She took a deep breath.

'From the deep of the sea, mermaid fire come to me!' she exclaimed.

She gasped. Her hands suddenly felt warm and tingling. The feeling spread up her arms and then a spark of green fire flowed out of the rock. She caught it in the palms of her hands and it formed into a glowing ball about the size of her thumbnail.

She swam to the surface. 'I've got some! I've got some!'

All around her, other people in her class were surfacing too, their hands outstretched, all holding tiny green balls. Electra felt a flash of disappointment. She'd thought that she was going to be the only person to have collected some, but everyone had managed it and some people had got even more than her.

'Well done, everyone. Bring the fire over here,' Solon instructed, holding out an empty conch shell for the fire to be put into. 'And then try again, and

see if you can get a bit more. Remember the deeper you go, the more fire you will collect.'

Electra swam over with the others and put her fire in the conch shell. Her friends all headed back to the reef but she hesitated. She didn't want to get just a tiny bit again. She wanted to get

a great big ball of fire. She glanced away from the reef, an idea coming into her mind.

If she swam right out, she could dive down and collect fire there. She would be bound to get loads more than anyone else if she went all the way down to the seabed. She imagined herself coming up with a huge ball of fire. She could almost see the amazement on Solon's face and hear his words of praise.

She made up her mind. *I'll do it!* she thought.

She plunged under the water and

began swimming away from the others. She didn't stop until she was sure she was far out. She surfaced and looked back. The reef, Solon and the others seemed a long way away.

Here goes, Electra decided, with a shiver of excitement. She dived down. At first the sea was clear and warm, but as she went deeper and deeper, the water got darker and colder.

Where's the bottom? Electra thought, straining her eyes through the gloom. She swallowed, feeling a sudden shiver of something very like fear. She'd never been so deep before. She wondered if she were in the twilight zone. Maris had told her about the twilight zone. It was where the water was so deep that the sunlight couldn't reach down through it. Maris had said that most merpeople avoided the twilight zone. Stories about the strange creatures that were supposed

to lurk on the seabed there flashed into Electra's mind – gulper eels with huge mouths, viperfish with long sharp teeth, giant squid with trailing poisonous tentacles. She peered downwards. Beneath her, things were moving – large shadowy shapes . . .

Suddenly something grabbed one of her arms. It started pulling her down!

Chapter Three

Electra gasped and struggled. The thing seemed to tangle further round her. It felt like a tentacle. Maybe it was a giant squid, trying to pull her into its underwater cave.

'No!' Electra cried, a wave of panic

sweeping over her. Yanking her arms this way and that, she fought desperately. The water was black all around her and there seemed to be things everywhere, grasping at her and tangling round her arms and hair.

Electra pulled herself free, and turned and kicked towards the surface as fast as she could.

She swam and swam, her heart pounding in her chest. Reaching the surface, she burst through. The sunlight seemed to hit her in the face. She looked around fearfully, half expecting to see a giant squid or some other sort of terrifying sea monster shooting up beside her, but there was nothing. Still, she wasn't going to hang around.

She plunged towards the reef and raced back to the safety of the shallower waters.

Sam was the first person she reached.

'Hi, Electra!' he exclaimed, holding up a small ball of green fire. 'Isn't this fun!' His voice faltered as he took in Electra's wide eyes and scared face. 'What . . . what's the matter?' he asked in alarm. 'You look frightened!'

Electra swallowed. She was never frightened of anything. All her friends thought she was really brave. She couldn't tell Sam about what had happened. With a huge effort, she forced a smile on to her face. 'Me? Frightened! Of course not!' she lied.

Sam didn't look convinced, but just then Sasha swam over with two of their other friends, Hakim and Nerissa.

'Have you been diving down far out in the deep sea?' asked Hakim, his brown eyes wide. 'Sasha said you were going to try.'

'You're so brave, Electra,' Nerissa gasped. 'No one else would dare to do that.'

Seeing the admiration on her friends' faces, Electra just couldn't

admit to them how frightened she had just been. She really liked her friends thinking she was brave.

'So, what was it like down there?' Hakim went on.

'Did you see any sea monsters?' Nerissa asked.

'No,' Electra replied. 'But . . . but I saw the caves where they lived,' she invented quickly as she saw Nerissa and Hakim start to look disappointed. 'And there were loads of other things. Sea dragons and really scary things, but I wasn't frightened at all.'

'Wow!' Sasha, Nerissa and Hakim breathed.

'Electra,' Sam said slowly, 'if you went all the way to the seabed, why haven't you got any fire with you?'

Electra felt her face go red. 'I . . . I forgot. I was so busy looking at everything down there.' Then she added, 'But I could have got loads of fire if I'd wanted.'

To her relief, just at that moment, Solon clapped his hands. 'Right, Class Four!' he called. 'Come over here!'

Avoiding Sam's eyes, Electra swam over to Solon's side.

'You've all been doing very well at collecting fire,' Solon said, looking pleased. 'So, I think we'll have a competition. I want you to get into teams of five and I'm going to give you one hour to collect mermaid fire. The team with the most fire at the end of an hour wins.'

'Will there be prizes?' Nerissa asked eagerly.

Solon nodded. 'Yes. There will be prizes.'

Sam, Sasha, Nerissa, Hakim and Electra immediately formed a team. 'This is brilliant!' Hakim said excitedly. 'We're bound to win with Electra in our team!'

'Yeah!' Nerissa put in. 'You can dive down really deep again, Electra, and get loads of fire.'

'Yeah,' Electra faltered. Dive down really deep! She definitely didn't want to do that.

'Let's get started,' Sasha said.

They all plunged downwards into

the water. Electra froze. What was she going to do? Her friends were expecting her to dive down into the deep sea again, but she couldn't. She just couldn't. She imagined those horrible tentacles closing round her wrists, pulling her down towards the seabed, down and down . . .

Sam and Sasha surfaced. They each

had a small green ball of fire in their hands. 'What are you doing, Electra?' Sasha asked in surprise. 'Why aren't you collecting fire?'

'I'm just going to,' Electra lied, feeling sick. 'I'm . . . I'm just deciding the best place to dive from.' She saw Sam start to frown. 'I'll . . . er . . . be back soon,' she said. And before he could say anything, she plunged away into the sea.

She swam until she was a good distance from them and then stopped. OK, so now what was she going to do?

Chapter Four

There was a splash in the water and a grey head surfaced, the mouth opening in a wide dolphin grin. 'Splash!' Electra exclaimed in surprise. 'What are you doing here? I thought you'd gone home.'

Splash shook his head. 'I didn't go through the gate. I just hung around by the reef,' he said. 'Don't worry, though, Solon hasn't seen me. I've kept out of his way.'

Electra stroked his smooth head. She was very glad to see him. 'Oh, Splash,' she sighed. 'I'm in real trouble.'

Splash looked at her curiously. 'What's wrong? I thought you weren't looking happy. That's why I came over.'

Electra knew she could tell Splash anything and he wouldn't laugh at

her or stop being her friend.

'I went diving . . .' she began, and then told him the whole story about how she had got frightened and come back to the surface. 'Now I'm too scared to dive down again,' she finished off. 'But everyone's expecting me to and I don't know what to do. I don't want to tell them I'm scared.'

Splash's black eyes looked confused. 'They wouldn't mind. They're your friends.'

'But they think I'm really brave. They think I've been to the bottom already and . . .' Electra's voice faltered as her worst fear rushed out, 'and they might not like me any more if they find out I've lied and that I was frightened! I've got to get some fire from the seabed, Splash. Lots of it.'

Splash thought for a moment, his head to one side. 'I know,' he said suddenly. 'How about I dive down for you?'

'But dolphins can't collect mermaid fire,' Electra pointed out.

'Yes, but I could find a safe place for you to dive down to,' Splash said. 'I can go down to the bottom and check it's safe. Then you can follow me, collect some fire and come back.'

Electra frowned. She didn't like the idea at all. 'But what if something happens to you when you dive down? There were all sorts of shadows moving around near the bottom, and there was that thing that grabbed me. What if it gets you?'

Splash shrugged. 'I'll be careful and

I can swim faster than you.'

'It's too dangerous . . .' Electra protested.

But Splash ignored her. 'Don't worry. I'll see you in a bit,' he said. Flipping downwards, he dived towards the bottom of the ocean before she could stop him.

'Splash!' Electra gasped. But he had

already vanished from sight.

Heart racing, Electra bobbed to the surface. What was she going to do?

'Hey! Is that dolphin yours?'

Electra swung round. The Year Seven mermaid with the blonde plait had seen her and was swimming towards her. Electra nodded, her mind whirling. All she could think

about was the fact that Splash had dived down to the seabed. He might well be in danger.

'Well, don't let him dive too far down,' the older mermaid warned. 'There's a forest of giant sea firs on the seabed just below here.'

'Sea firs?' Electra echoed. 'What are they?'

'They look like trees but they're actually a type of sea creature. They've got tentacles instead of branches. Their tentacles wrap round anything they touch. It's not so bad for merpeople – we can use our hands to untangle ourselves, but dolphins get completely tangled up.'

Electra stared at her in horror. That must have been what grabbed her before. But what about Splash? If he got tangled up he wouldn't be able to get back to the surface, and dolphins couldn't stay underwater forever. They needed to come back to the surface to breathe or they would drown.

'But . . . but . . .' she stammered. However, the older mermaid didn't hear her; she was already hurrying back to her friends.

Electra didn't know what to do. *Maybe I should go and get Solon*, she thought desperately. But Solon was all the way over by the reef. It would take ages to reach him. She looked after the older mermaid. She had reached her friends now, and they were already

heading off swiftly through the waves, their tails letting them swim far faster than she could ever hope to go with her two legs.

Electra's heart pounded. There was no one around. What was she going to do?

She looked at the deep water. Fear raced through her at the thought of swimming to the seabed, but Splash was in trouble. He needed her. Electra knew she didn't have a choice. Taking a deep breath, she dived down.

Chapter Five

Down and down Electra went, hardly noticing as the waters changed from turquoise to dark blue. Where was Splash? She kicked onwards, her eyes straining through the gathering gloom.

At last, she reached a point where she could hardly see at all. The water was very cold. 'Splash!' she shouted, trying to ignore the flickers of shadowy movement beneath her. The seabed with its strange inhabitants must be just down there. 'Splash, where are you?' she yelled.

'Electra!'

Hearing Splash's familiar whistle, Electra's heart leapt.

'I'm over here! I'm all tangled up in something,' Splash called from a little way off. Electra swam towards the sound of his voice. Suddenly, in the gloom, she saw a dolphin-shaped shadow struggling to pull free from a mass of rope-like tentacles.

Electra remembered what the older mermaid had said. 'You've got caught in a giant sea fir,' she said. 'Hold still, I'll try and untangle you.'

She started to pull at the tentacles,

but it was too dark to see what she was doing and Splash only seemed to get more and more tangled up. It didn't help that all the time Electra kept imagining things creeping up on them – big hungry things. Her fingers fumbled with the tentacles.

'I can't do it!' she exclaimed in

frustration. 'I can't see anything.'

'What about getting some mermaid fire?' Splash suggested. 'If you get some of that you'll be able to see.'

'But there's no coral this far down and the only other place I can get it from is the seabed,' Electra told him. She looked downwards. The shadows were still moving in a sinister way.

'Electra, I'm going to need some more air soon,' Splash said, sounding worried.

Electra knew she had no choice. She would have to go down to the seabed for some fire to see by. 'OK,' she told Splash. 'I'll be back in a minute.' Screwing up all her courage, she dived down towards the dark seabed.

Her hands touched sand and rock. She was at the bottom! 'From the deep of the sea, mermaid fire come to me,' she gasped.

A wave of warmth swept over her from her head down to her toes. Her fingers tingled and then suddenly, from the rock, came a flood of green fire. More and

more of it, until Electra had a
huge glowing ball in her
hands.

'Oh, wow!' she gasped as light
sparked off the ball.

Looking up, she saw Splash caught
in the red tentacles of the sea fir.
Swimming up to him, she placed the
ball under one arm and began to pull

the tentacles away. When the stubborn ones rewound about him, she touched them with the ball of fire and they instantly drew back. 'That's it!' she exclaimed at last.

'I'm free!' Splash cried, plunging away from the sea fir. 'Thanks, Electra!'

Electra felt a wave of relief. 'Come on,' she said. 'Let's get back to the surface.'

'Hang on,' Splash said. 'Have you seen what it's like down here? Look around. It's amazing!'

Electra looked and her eyes

widened. She'd been so busy thinking about Splash that she hadn't noticed what the bottom of the sea looked like, but now she could see that Splash was right. It was incredible. There were strange twisty rocks covered with living sponges in different shades of purple, orange, pink and yellow. Giant blue basket sponges

with mouths as big as a person jutted upwards, and all around them were shoals of green and turquoise fish. They had huge eyes and underbellies that flashed and sparkled with glowing lights. Beside them, glass jellyfish with long tentacles floated, their see-through bodies lit up with bright displays of rainbow-coloured lights as they drifted in and out of the enormous

red sea firs that grew majestically out of the sand.

'Wow!' Electra gasped. Now she had light to see by, the seabed didn't seem scary any more. It looked beautiful and mysterious and she wanted to explore it.

Splash seemed to read her thoughts. 'Come along, let's have a look around,' he urged.

'But don't you need to surface for some air?' Electra asked anxiously.

'I'll be OK for a while,' Splash replied. 'I want to explore.'

Electra didn't need any more

persuading and the two of them swam on, weaving through the craggy rocks.

'Look, there's a shipwreck!' Electra said suddenly.

She and Splash swam towards the old ship. It was covered in sea anemones, their white fronds waving in the water. As they peered in through the windows an enormous

greeny-grey octopus swam out. Electra and Splash jumped back, but it just peered at them curiously with its large eyes and then waved a tentacle gently at them before swimming on its way.

Leaving the wreck, Electra and Splash swam with the shoals of magical glowing fish and played a quick game of tag with a huge stripy eel.

'This is fantastic!' Electra said as they swished through the water, the glow from the ball of mermaid fire lighting their way. 'I never knew the bottom of the sea was like this. It's not frightening at all.'

'I know. It's great!' Splash agreed. 'But we should start going back now. I'm going to need some air soon.'

Electra nodded and, tightly clutching the huge ball of mermaid fire, she followed Splash up to the surface.

They reached the surface and looked at each other. 'Wow!' Electra said, shaking the water out of her eyes. 'Just wait till the others hear about this!'

Just then there was the sound of a

large gong being banged. 'Five minutes left!' came Solon's faint shout from around the reef. 'Five minutes to go in the mermaid-fire competition!'

Electra gasped. The competition! She'd almost forgotten about it! 'I'd better get back to the reef!'

'Grab hold of my fin,' Splash said. 'I'll pull you through the water. It'll be quicker that way.'

Electra didn't need telling twice. She grabbed Splash's fin with one hand and held on to the enormous ball of fire with the other. 'Come on, Splash!' she cried. 'Let's go!'

Chapter Six

Electra gasped when the spray from the waves hit her in the face as she and Splash zoomed through the water towards the others. Sam, Sasha, Nerissa and Hakim were swimming in the shallower water near the reef.

'Electra, where have you been?' Nerissa exclaimed as Splash swooshed to a stop.

'You've been gone ages,' Sasha said. 'We were really worried about you.'

'Yeah,' Sam said. 'Look, if you don't

want to dive –' He broke off as Electra lifted the glowing ball of fire out of the water. 'Oh, wow!' he gasped.

The others stared as if they couldn't believe their eyes.

Electra grinned. 'I told you I'd get some fire.'

'So, you really went down to the seabed?' Sam asked.

'I told him you would,' Hakim said. 'Sam thought you were scared to dive down. But the rest of us knew you wouldn't be scared. You're not frightened of anything.'

Sam looked shamefaced. 'I'm sorry, Electra,' he said. 'I should have known you wouldn't be scared.'

Electra hesitated. Should she let them carry on believing she was brave or should she tell them all the truth? Before she could decide, Solon banged the gong again. 'Thirty seconds left!'

'Quick!' Sasha exclaimed. 'We must get this fire to Solon or we'll lose the competition! Hurry, Electra!'

Electra was already moving. She grabbed Splash's fin. 'Let's go, Splash!'

Splash raced over to the reef. There were five large conch shells on top of the reef and Solon was standing beside them. The shells were filled

with all the mermaid fire that the five teams had collected.

'Electra!' Solon exclaimed as Electra and Splash swooshed to a stop, sending up a spray of water. 'Why is Splash here? I thought I told you to send him home. I –' He broke off as Electra pulled the ball of fire out of the waves. He stared at it. 'Oh, my goodness! Where did you get that?'

'From the seabed out in the deep sea,' Electra replied.

'From the seabed in the deep sea!' Solon echoed. 'Electra! Mermaids your age aren't supposed to swim that far down. There are all sorts of things that could trap a young mermaid down there.'

'It's wonderful,' Electra said, her eyes shining as she remembered what it was like at the bottom of the sea.

'Wonderful!' Solon exclaimed.

Electra grinned. Before Solon could say any more on the subject she held out the mermaid fire. 'Can I add this

to my team's collection, Solon?'

Solon looked at her rather dazedly and then turned to the shells. 'You know, I . . . I don't think it will fit.'

Electra looked at him eagerly. 'So, does that mean my team are the winners, then?'

'Yes.' Solon nodded weakly. 'I rather think it does.'

'Hurray!' shouted Sam, Sasha, Nerissa and Hakim, who had arrived just in time to hear what Solon said.

The rest of the class had now noticed the ball of fire and were all swimming over, wanting to know how Electra had collected so much. She started telling them about the bottom of the sea, only breaking off when Solon banged his gong.

'Quiet please, class! It's time to

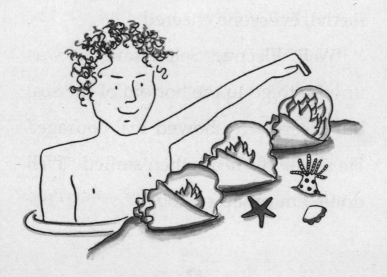

announce the winners of the mermaid-fire competition. They are Electra, Sam, Sasha, Nerissa and Hakim. Would they please come forward and collect their prizes!'

The rest of the class clapped as Electra and her friends went forward. They were each presented with a shell medal. When Electra collected her medal, everyone cheered.

'Well, Electra,' Solon said, 'it was unwise to go to the bottom of the sea, but it certainly showed real courage.' He shook his head, then smiled. 'Well done. I'm proud of you.'

Electra glowed with delight. For once, she wasn't getting told off!

Solon turned back to the others. 'And now,' he said, 'it's lunchtime. I'll see you all back in school this afternoon.'

As everyone started to swim away, Electra joined her friends.

'We did it!' Nerissa exclaimed. 'We won!'

'And it's all thanks to you, Electra,' Sasha cried. 'You're so brave.'

Looking at her friends' admiring faces, Electra knew she couldn't lie any longer. 'I'm not,' she said. 'I'm really not. I . . . I was scared of diving that deep. I only went because Splash needed me.'

The others stared in astonishment.

'What are you talking about?' Nerissa asked.

'I was caught in a sea fir near the bottom,' Splash explained. 'Electra swam down to save me.'

Electra took a deep breath and then told them the whole story. It was hard, but she had to tell her friends the truth. As she finished she hung her head, hardly daring to meet their eyes. 'So you see, Sam was right all along,' she said in a small voice. 'I was frightened. I'm not actually brave at all.'

'But you are!' Sam exclaimed. Electra looked up at him. He was staring at her with admiration. 'You

were scared but you still dived down to help Splash. That was a really brave thing to do, Electra.'

Hakim nodded. 'I think it's the bravest thing I've ever heard.'

'Splash might have drowned if it hadn't been for you, Electra,' Sasha said.

'You're amazing!' Nerissa told her.

Electra felt as if a huge weight had

rolled off her shoulders. She smiled at her friends and then everyone hugged.

'So, what was the bottom of the sea like?' Hakim asked eagerly.

'Brilliant!' Electra said, her eyes glowing as she remembered. 'You'll all have to dive down with me one day and see it too.'

'No way!' Sasha exclaimed.

'It's much too scary for me,' Nerissa said.

'Me too,' Sam agreed. 'You can have the adventures for all of us, Electra.'

Electra smiled. That suited her just fine. After all, she wouldn't be totally on her own. She knew she had one friend who would always come with her, no matter what she wanted to do.

Almost as though he was reading her mind, Splash swam up beside her and butted her shoulder with his nose.

'We will have more adventures together, won't we, Electra?' he said hopefully.

Electra hugged him. 'Oh, yes,' she said happily. 'We will!'

Do you love magic, unicorns and fairies?

Join the sparkling

Linda Chapman

fan club today!

It's FREE!

You will receive a sparkle pack, including:

Stickers   **Badge**

Membership card   **Glittery pencil**

Plus four Linda Chapman newsletters every year,
packed full of fun, games, news and competitions.
And look out for a special card on your birthday!

How to join:

Visit lindachapman.co.uk and enter your details

Send your name, address, date of birth* and email address (if you have one) to:
**Linda Chapman Fan Club, Puffin Marketing,
80 Strand, London, WC2R 0RL**